ONE
MORE
GIFT TO
GIVE

May the true gifts of Christmas —
family, faith and friendship —
always be yours.

John Shaughnessy

ONE MORE GIFT TO GIVE

John Shaughnessy

Saint Catherine of Siena Press
Indianapolis

Saint Catherine of Siena Press
4812 North Park Avenue
Indianapolis, IN 46205
888-232-1492
www.saintcatherineofsienapress.com
www.onemoregifttogive.com

To order additional copies of this book:
contact Theological Book Service at 888-544-8674

Printed in the United States of America.

ISBN-13: 978-0-9762284-5-5
ISBN-10: 0-9762284-5-9
Library of Congress Control Number: 2006931479

Acknowledgments may be found on page 61.

Cover design by Joseph Sadlier

Back cover photograph by Frank Espich

To my Mom and Dad,
who always give their children and grandchildren
the greatest gifts of Christmas —
love, faith, and family

To my brother and my sisters,
who share the memories of our childhood and
the bonds that still connect us

To my children,
who have touched my life with so much magic and joy

And to my wife,
my best friend,
who always gives from her heart

⋆ ONE ⋆

He always hated taking off the suit for the last time.

Sure, it meant a welcome rest from the long lines, the endless letters, and all the pressure of trying to make Christmas just right for so many people. And he was always thankful when he didn't have to hear *I Saw Mommy Kissing Santa Claus* for another eleven months.

Yet there was something about wearing that red-and-white suit that made the world view him differently. Nearly everyone smiled at him and expected the best of him. And when you had a child who believed in you and trusted you from the deepest reaches of his or her heart, well, there was just no better feeling in the world.

But even that feeling didn't completely explain why he hated taking off the suit for the last time. Wearing the suit didn't just change people's views of him; it changed his view of the world.

Like the time he slipped into his Santa suit on Christmas Eve and decided he wanted to do more than deliver toys to families. That night, he loaded up the food and the clothes he had collected. Then he and his helpers visited Christmas tree lots, getting great bargains for the Charlie Brown-type trees no one else wanted. And when he headed into a poor neighborhood and didn't see a Christmas tree in a front window, he stopped and gave the people a tree and whatever toys and clothes the children needed. Or the time he was sitting in a shopping center and he noticed a little girl hesitate as she approached him. He could see that her shyness was different than the usual child's nervousness about meeting a huge, bearded man in a red-and-white suit. There were so many things she wanted to tell him, but she wasn't sure he would understand her— because she was deaf.

Then the little girl's greatest wish came true. He was using sign language for her. For her! Her eyes widened with the Christmas wonder all children deserve to experience. Catching her breath, she told him she wanted a puppy. Then she ran to her mother and told her that Santa understood her; Santa had talked to her! And he tried to hide the tears that the girl's mother couldn't.

Wearing the suit, he had seen the tears of too many children, like those from broken homes who asked him for the only wish that mattered to them: having their fathers back at home with them. Yet while he tried to soothe the children's tears and fears, his suit didn't have the magical power to make everything perfect. And sometimes the sadness overwhelmed him.

So it was this holiday season with a six-year-old boy who was very ill, a child he was supposed to visit in the hospital on Christmas Day. But the boy's parents phoned him a few weeks before Christmas, desperately asking him to come sooner. The doctor had just told the parents to savor their time with their son because there was nothing more she could do for him.

The boy smiled when he arrived the next day, reaching up to touch his velvet-and-fur suit. All through the visit, he stayed jolly for the boy, wanting to give the child a feeling of warmth and happiness. Yet when he left the hospital, he couldn't hold back the tears. He leaned against a wall for support as the snow began to fall, the snowflakes settling on his red hat and suit. He cried so hard he began shaking. He reacted the same way the next day when he phoned the hospital to check on the boy and learned the child had died.

On this Christmas morning, he sat in his chair at home, tugging at his shiny black boots, his red-and-white hat already tossed on the floor. He was so tired he could have just fallen into bed with his suit on to begin the long winter's nap he deserved. But another memory crossed his mind, recharging him.

It was the memory of a boy who was twelve then—an age when it wasn't good enough for the boy to doubt the existence of Santa Claus; he wanted to prove it to others. So after his parents went to bed, the boy took off his socks and hung one on the fireplace, smugly figuring he would have the proof he needed by morning. Yet when the boy came down the stairs that Christmas morning, he found a candy cane and a note signed "Santa" in his sock. And his parents were still asleep.

That memory made him smile as he slipped off his boots. He took the candy canes from his pockets and flicked some cookie crumbs from his suit. In that moment, he thought about all the children who had come to him with their hopes, their dreams, and their desires.

While exhaustion seeped into every part of his body, he still wasn't willing to give into it. There was just so much he loved about this season. Every time he put on the suit, he saw the gift of hope, the beauty of dreams, the wonder of the world. Every time he put on the suit, he was reminded of how much so many people take for granted: the blessing of health, the love of family, and the fulfillment of faith.

He knew he should get some sleep. He rested his head against the white fur of his collar and he folded his hands against the red velvet of his coat. He told himself he would take off the suit in another minute. Yet the thought suddenly struck him that there was one more gift he had to give. He just wasn't sure what that gift was. So he slipped his shiny black boots on again. He reached for his red-and-white hat. Then he walked out the door toward a Christmas he would never forget.

⋆ Two ⋆

As Santa walked, a soft snow fell, illuminated by the glow of the streetlights in the early morning. Less than a mile away, Katie Sanders sat awake in bed while her husband, Joe, slept. She glanced at the alarm clock that read 6:23, knowing it was set to ring in seven minutes. She had already been up an hour, awakened by a nauseous feeling in her body. A strong strain of the stomach flu had swept through the community in the week before Christmas, leaving many of the children in her class sick. As a teacher, Katie usually was immune from catching the illnesses of her students, but apparently she hadn't escaped this time. Still, the physical aches didn't bother her as much this morning as the haunting memories of last Christmas. When she awakened on Christmas morning a year ago, she had never felt so much love, hope, and faith. Yet before that day ended, all those feelings had disappeared, replaced by a heartbreaking pain she still hadn't been able to overcome.

When the clock turned to 6:29, she switched off the alarm and began to gently nudge Joe to wake him. They had been married seven years. At their wedding, the long-time organist of Our Mother of Sorrows Church noticed the love they had for each other. Of course, most couples at their weddings reflect that love, but the organist, Mrs. Williams, saw something just a little more special about Katie and Joe. Since she was also the director of the church's Living Nativity, and since she was looking for a new young couple to play the roles of Mary and Joseph, Mrs. Williams approached Katie and Joe after church about a month after their wedding. Joe thought it was a great idea. Katie agreed, too. They had played the roles ever since, including last night—before, during, and after the midnight Mass. They had to do it again this morning, getting in place well before people started to arrive for the eight o'clock Mass.

Since they didn't get to bed until after 2 a.m., Katie had to nudge Joe again. She whispered in his ear that they would be late if they didn't leave soon. Joe sat up and slid his feet to the hardwood floor. When Katie did the same, the nausea hit her again. She held her hand against her forehead, which Joe noticed as he slipped into his insulated underwear. It was part of the layers of protection they had learned to use to fight the December chill while they posed in the outdoor stable. Joe asked Katie if she was okay. She said "yes" even though her body felt differently. She knew she had to be in the stable to make the scene of the first Christmas complete. In seven years of playing the role of Mary, she often thought about the real mother of Jesus. She knew that Mary never thought of herself first. She knew the hardships and sacrifices that Mary endured for her son and her God.

While Katie dressed, Joe walked down the steps and through the back door to warm the car. When he saw the snow, he smiled, being one of those people who believe there is something just a little more special about a white Christmas. He turned on the heater in the car and swept snow from the windows with a small blue brush. When he heard the back door close, he turned and looked at Katie. The light from the patio shined on her, illuminating her rosy cheeks, her soft brown eyes, and the hints of gold in her shoulder-length, brownish-blonde hair. Her beauty always mesmerized him. But the light also showed the sadness etched in her face. There was a time in their lives when he could chase away her sadness with one of his jokes or a crazy stunt. But that time had passed, and he knew it had everything to do with what happened last Christmas.

Silently, they drove along the streets of their town where many of the houses were aglow with outdoor Christmas lights, flashing red, green, white, and blue in the morning darkness. A large, wooden Santa stood atop one of the roofs, with a sign next to it, trimmed in white lights, that read, "Welcome, Santa!" Two blocks later, another house featured a small Nativity scene in the front yard. As they stopped for a red traffic light, they looked toward a corner house where someone had just flicked on the lights of a Christmas tree inside. When the traffic light turned green,

Joe continued to admire the Christmas decorations in the neighborhood. Then he saw a man in a Santa suit walking along the street, bathed in the glow of a streetlight. Pointing him out to Katie, Joe didn't notice the pothole in the middle of the street. As the left front tire crashed into the deep hole, it rocked the car and jolted Katie and Joe. It also left the tire flat. Joe knew they didn't have time to change the tire. Fortunately, they were just three blocks from the church. As they set out, walking in the falling snow, Joe pushed his hands into the pockets of his Navy pea coat while Katie wrapped a royal blue scarf around her hair. Neither of them talked.

When they reached the church, Joe saw a scrawled note on the wooden door of the dressing area leading to the outdoor stable. The note was from Father Angelos, the pastor of the church. The note read, "I've been called to give last rites to Mrs. Moriarty. I'll be back as soon as I can." Inside the dressing area, Katie and Joe hung their coats on hooks and changed into the worn, rough clothes of Joseph and Mary. After slipping into Mary's clothes, Katie picked up the life-like doll that represented the baby Jesus.

Stepping into the stable always made Katie think of how this was the way it must have begun for Mary, Joseph, and Jesus—the three of them starting off together in a moment that would change each of their lives forever, a moment that would also change the world forever. Walking toward the manger, Katie was surprised to see a fresh set of small footprints in the snow. She also noticed a brown blanket covering the manger where she would place the doll. When she knelt to pick up the blanket, she gasped and then shouted, "Oh my God!"

⋆ THREE ⋆

Two blocks south of the church, Jack Warren stopped his yellow cab at a red light. Looking through the windshield, he noticed the snow falling heavier. As the owner of the Triple Crown Cab Company, Jack had always worked the 8 p.m. to 8 a.m. shift on Christmas Eve and Christmas morning as a cab driver. He did it so his regular drivers could enjoy

Christmas at home with their families. Jack also did it because of what had happened about fifty years ago on Christmas Eve. The incident first taught him about the hope and joy that Christmas could bring to people. In a way, Jack had been searching to recapture those feelings ever since.

While that moment had never been repeated, Jack had never regretted taking the twelve-hour shift every year. Besides helping his employees, he had made Christmas better for others: driving older people to church or rushing last-minute travelers from the bus station or the airport to their homes. He never got tired of watching people dart from his cab into the arms of family and friends.

Then there were the times he picked up people who drank too much in bars on Christmas Eve. He always listened to their stories of having no one to share Christmas with, and how they dreaded being alone on this day of faith and family. When he reached their dark houses or apartments, he always made sure they got into their homes safely. He also never charged anyone a fare during this shift. He always figured it was his way of giving a Christmas gift to others.

As the windshield wipers of his cab swept away the snow, Jack looked at the clock on the dashboard that read 6:57. The traffic light was still red. He hadn't had anyone in his cab since he drove home Mr. and Mrs. Moore, an elderly couple, from the midnight service at their church on the other side of town. He also knew that at this hour, on this day, he wasn't likely to get another passenger before his shift ended. Most people were at home with their loved ones. He could easily have gone home, too. Yet all his years in the taxi business had given him a sense of duty to the one customer who still could need a ride during his shift. Besides, he had no one waiting for him at home.

When the light switched to green, Jack turned left onto the street that led to Our Mother of Sorrows Church. Ever since the church started its Living Nativity, Jack had made a point of viewing the scene on Christmas morning. As an immigrant who came from Ireland to America by ship, Jack knew what it was like to come to a new place as a stranger, with just the clothes you were wearing and not enough money to find a decent place to sleep or stay. He had also always been drawn to the Living Nativity because of the sense of comfort he found in that scene.

"I need that comfort now more than ever," he told himself, running his right hand through his thinning silver hair.

✳ FOUR ✳

Anne Nelson locked the front door of her two-story, red-brick house and walked along a path that cut through the large yard toward the detached garage. The yard was filled with evergreens of increasing height, their limbs collecting the falling snow. She knew the snow would slow her drive to the hospital and make her even later for her shift that started at 7 a.m. Being late for work was something she had never done in her 23 years of nursing. Yet, for a moment this Christmas morning, she considered not going to work at all. She still hadn't shaken the feeling of having another child die on the pediatric intensive care unit, the most recent death having taken place just a few weeks ago. She told herself she had seen too many children die through the years. It's time to quit, she thought. Hitting her even harder was the reality that this was the first Christmas morning of the past twenty-two years that she didn't wake up next to Jeff, her husband, who died unexpectedly of a heart attack in October. She had spent the past hour thinking of him as she sat alone crying, in the dark, while she looked through the bay window at the evergreens. The only reason she didn't stay home was because she wanted to check on one of her patients, a six-year-old named Sally who had to stay in the hospital on Christmas.

Arriving at the hospital, Anne took the elevator to the pediatric intensive care unit and went immediately to Sally's room. Anne tiptoed to the bedside, and seeing that Sally was asleep, gently touched her short, dark-brown hair. After checking the girl's medical chart, she slipped out of the room and headed toward the nurse's station. Halfway there, she met Dr. Lanzinger, Sally's cardiologist, walking down the hall.

"Merry Christmas, Doctor," she whispered with a smile. "What are you doing here so early on Christmas morning?"

"I just wanted to check on Sally before I headed to my son's house to watch my grandkids open their gifts," the doctor said.

"It looks like she had a good night," Anne said. "She looks peaceful."

"That's good news. Thanks, Anne. Merry Christmas."

At the nurses' station, two other nurses had already arrived. They all wished each other a Merry Christmas. Then the phone rang. A supervisor said that one of the nurses in the emergency room had called in sick so another nurse was needed there. Anne volunteered, telling the other nurses that she began her career in the emergency room. She didn't tell them what she was also thinking: "This will be my last day at the hospital. I might as well end my time here in the same place where I started."

✶ FIVE ✶

When Joe heard Katie scream in the stable, he rushed toward her and found her kneeling in front of the manger. Looking down, he suddenly understood why she had yelled. Inside the brown blanket was a real baby. Even more unsettling, the child was barely breathing and there was a hint of blue in the baby's skin color. Katie wrapped the brown blanket around the child and rose quickly to her feet. She and Joe knew they had to get help immediately. But their car had a flat tire, their cell phones were at home, and there was no way of knowing when Father Angelos would return.

"Let's get to the street," Joe said. "We'll flag down a car and get a ride to the hospital."

They rushed to the deserted street. Looking up and down the road, Katie and Joe searched for any sign of a coming car. They saw none.

"Come on! Somebody come! Somebody come!" Joe shouted.

He was stunned when he saw a car turning onto the street, heading right toward them.

"It's a cab!" Joe yelled. He dashed into the middle of the road to stop the taxi.

Jack Warren couldn't believe the sight that appeared ahead of him. At first, the cab driver wondered if the combination of the falling snow and his lack of sleep had made him see things. Then he saw his eyes hadn't betrayed him. A wild-looking, bearded young man, dressed in a faded brown robe, stood in the middle of the street, waving frantically at him. By the curb was a young woman, dressed in similar clothes, looking panic-stricken as she held a bundle in her arms, against her chest.

"Holy Mother of God," Jack whispered in his Irish brogue as he stopped the cab on the snowy street, nearly hitting Joe.

Joe flung open the front passenger door and blurted, "You have to help us. We just found a baby. We need to get him to a hospital right away."

Looking at the crazed man, Jack thought of driving away. Then Katie lowered her head toward the cab. Her eyes flashed a fear that melted the cab driver's heart.

"Get in," Jack said.

As the young couple held the baby in the back seat, Jack rushed toward Mercy Hospital, knowing it was about a mile and a half straight ahead. He benefited from having the only car on the road, but the snow had turned even heavier, making the drive treacherous. Still, he pushed down the gas pedal when he heard the young woman begging in a soft whisper, "Breathe. Please! Breathe!"

Finally, he pulled the car in front of the emergency room entrance. The young couple ran from the cab and through the doors just as a man dressed in a Santa suit entered. Inside the emergency room, Anne Nelson turned toward the door. For a moment, the nurse wondered if the scene was orchestrated, with Santa, Mary, Joseph, and the Baby Jesus arriving together. Maybe this was the hospital's attempt to bring Christmas cheer to the staff that had to work Christmas morning, she thought. Then she saw the panic and the pleading in the eyes of the young woman who rushed toward her, holding out the baby.

Outside the emergency room, Jack slumped forward, his head against the steering wheel of his cab. He could feel his heart pounding beneath his kelly green jacket. A nurse leaving the hospital after her shift saw him slumped against the steering wheel. She knocked on the driver's side window but Jack didn't hear it. The nurse knocked harder. Finally, Jack raised his head and turned toward the window.

"Are you okay?" he heard the nurse say.

He nodded his head as he rolled down the window.

"Are you okay?" the nurse asked again.

"I'm fine," Jack said. "It's just been a long night. Thanks for stopping. Merry Christmas."

"Merry Christmas," the nurse replied.

As the nurse walked away, she pulled the hood of her light blue parka onto her head. Jack watched her for a moment as the cold air and snow surged through the open window, reviving him. He looked toward the entrance of the emergency room, thinking how much he hated hospitals. It was the last place he wanted to be on any day, let alone Christmas. But he felt drawn to know what would happen to the baby. He decided to park the cab in a nearby lot and check on the child.

The man in the Santa suit felt drawn to the child, too. When he first left his home this morning, he had no idea where he was headed. Yet when the snow started to fall, he saw the flakes on his red-and-white suit and immediately thought of the boy he had visited in the hospital in early December. He remembered how the child had reached up to touch him. He remembered the snow was still falling that day when he left the hospital. He remembered how hard he had cried that day in the snow. So he began walking toward the hospital, even though it was nearly two miles from his home. He didn't know what he would find or do when he reached the hospital. He just knew one lesson from all his years of celebrating Christmas and trying to make the season better for others: When you follow your heart, amazing things can happen. And when he reached the emergency room entrance at the same time that the Mary and Joseph look-a-likes arrived with a baby in a blanket, he believed his heart had led him to the right place.

"Maybe this child," he thought, "has something to do with the one gift I still need to give."

✳ SIX ✳

The baby stopped breathing right after Katie handed him to Anne Nelson. Anne also noticed the dusky blue tint of the baby's skin. She ran with him toward a room, calling to a young doctor and another nurse to help. The room soon filled with people who no longer thought about the hardship of working on Christmas. Everyone just focused on the newborn child—trying to get the baby to breathe, trying to get his body temperature back to normal.

In the waiting room, Katie, Joe, and the man in the Santa suit huddled in a corner. Joe and Katie had just finished giving all the information they had about the baby to an admissions clerk. The few other people in the emergency room's waiting area turned and stared at the three of them, shaking their heads in wonder. Katie and Joe didn't think about how odd it was that they were here with a stranger in a Santa suit. They were just worried about the baby. Besides, they saw something reassuring in the man's face and eyes, something comforting in his suit and his real white hair and beard. Holding hands, Katie and Joe began to pray. Santa lowered his head as the three of them asked God to let the baby live. When they finished, they saw Jack walking toward them. Beneath his silver hair, his ruddy face looked strained.

"How is the baby?" the cab driver asked softly.

"We haven't heard yet," Katie said, tears filling her eyes.

Joe put his arm around Katie's shoulder, drawing her close. When Katie stopped crying, Joe told her, "We should call Father Angelos to let him know why we aren't in the stable. I'll try to find a phone. I'll be back as soon as I can."

When Joe left, no one talked for a few moments. Then Santa, who never really saw the infant in the blanket, asked Katie, "How old is your baby?"

"I don't know. He's not ours," she said, leaning forward, cupping her face in her hands. "We found him this morning. Joe and I play Mary and Joseph in a Living Nativity at our church. The baby was in the manger in a blanket when we got there."

✶

She shared the details of how they rushed to the street with the child, how they prayed that some passing car would see them, and how the taxi suddenly appeared. She looked toward Jack, who had been pacing back and forth nervously. She realized she hadn't thanked him for stopping, nor paid him for the ride to the hospital.

"I can't thank you enough," she said. "How much do we owe you?"

"Nothing," he said.

"But you did so much," she said.

"It's fine. I just wanted to see if the baby was okay."

"Thank you. You're an angel," she replied. "I don't know what we would have done if you hadn't come along."

"When I first saw your husband in the middle of the street, he looked so wild I wasn't sure about stopping," Jack said.

"We must have looked like a sight," Katie said, wiping at her eyes.

"I was going to stop by the Living Nativity to say a prayer," Jack said. "I've always liked being there on Christmas morning. It just worked out."

At the front desk of the emergency room, a man in a rumpled gray coat approached the admissions clerk who had taken the information from Joe and Katie. The clerk had phoned the police to report the abandoned baby. Talking to her, Detective Mike Piersall combed his fingers through his windswept, dark-brown hair, trying to arrange it back into place. Lined with wrinkles, his face reflected the look of a man who had seen too much in life, most of it bad. He knew that reality didn't change for him on Christmas Day either. Last Christmas, he began the day in an alley where someone had been shot and left to die. He also investigated a burglary in which the thieves stole a family's Christmas gifts when the family went to church. Later that day, he was called to a house where a husband got drunk and beat his wife, pushing her into the Christmas tree while their children cowered in a corner. And this Christmas shift began in a hospital—his first stop in an investigation concerning an abandoned baby.

"Merry Christmas," he told himself.

He had already checked with the clerk to see if any woman had arrived at the emergency room to seek help for injuries related to giving birth. When she told him "no," he knew he would have to call or visit the other emergency rooms in the city. Then he asked the clerk to point out the people who brought in the baby.

When she did, he shook his head and smiled in spite of himself, in spite of all he knew about the horror of the world. In twenty-five years as a cop, Piersall thought he had seen everything. But seeing a guy in a Santa suit sitting next to Mary and Joseph was a new one for him. After he introduced himself, he sat across from Katie and Joe and questioned them about the baby. They shared every detail they knew, including the brown blanket. The detective made a mental note to get the blanket before he left the hospital.

"Did you see anyone around the Nativity scene or the church when you first got there?" Piersall asked.

"No," Joe said.

"But there was a fresh set of footprints leading up to the stable," Katie said.

"They've probably been covered by the falling snow, but I'll check it out," Piersall said. "Okay, that's all for now but I might need to talk to you later."

Getting up to leave, the detective thanked them. He also thought how good, how decent, they were.

"Merry Christmas," Katie said to the detective.

"Merry Christmas," said the man in the Santa suit.

"Merry Christmas," Piersall said.

It was the first time in a long while that the detective could remember saying those words sincerely.

Before he left the hospital, Piersall picked up the brown blanket from the clerk. He also told her he would call or stop by later to see if the baby was still alive.

⋆ SEVEN ⋆

In the emergency room, Anne and the young doctor rushed to put the baby on a ventilator. The infant started to breathe again but the heart monitor showed the baby still in distress. When she first carried the baby into the room, Anne felt a vibration across the boy's chest. She mentioned it to the doctor who had already placed a stethoscope on the baby's heart. Amid the baby's rapid heartbeat, the young doctor heard a loud swoosh, the sound of a heart murmur. He had never heard one so loud. The look he gave Anne frightened her.

"I saw Dr. Lanzinger in the hospital earlier this morning. Should I try to get him?" she asked, moving toward the phone.

"Yes," the young doctor said.

Dr. Lanzinger had just stepped off the elevator on the way to the parking garage when he received the call. Seconds later, he walked quickly into the emergency room, drawing the attention of Katie, Joe, Santa, and Jack.

"It's been almost a half-hour and we still haven't heard anything," Katie said, wringing her hands. "I just couldn't handle it…" She started to cry. "Not again."

Jack didn't know what Katie meant, but he realized they needed to do something to take her mind off the baby, especially since it could be a long time before they heard any news. In the empty seat next to him, he saw a newspaper article about Christmas stories. He turned to the man in the Santa suit and said, "I bet you have some great Christmas stories. Could you tell us a couple? To pass the time while we're waiting?"

"Sure," Santa said.

He began with the story of the twelve-year-old boy with the socks who wanted to prove that Santa Claus didn't exist.

"He was so sure of himself but he still couldn't get his parents to admit it," Santa said. "Parents are always the last ones who want to see the magic of Christmas disappear for their children. So hanging his white sock on the fireplace was his way of making his mom and dad admit it. A funny thing happened, though.

"When he woke up that Christmas morning, he went straight for the fireplace, smugly expecting the white sock to be empty. Yet when he reached for it, he felt something inside. He pulled out the candy cane first. He didn't know what to think. Then he noticed there was still something else inside the sock. This time, he pulled out a note that was folded several times. When he unfolded it, there was a message for him."

"What did it say?" Joe asked as Jack and Katie looked up at Santa.

"It said, *'Believe. Believe in the magic of the season. Believe you have a gift to make the world better.'* It was signed, 'Santa.' The boy didn't know what to think. No one else was awake in the house. And he didn't recognize the writing as coming from either of his parents. He kept reading the note over and over. *'Believe.'* He was stunned and amazed."

"Were you the one who left the candy cane and the note?" Jack asked.

"No," Santa said.

"Then who did? The parents?" Joe asked.

"I don't know," Santa said. "I've never figured it out. I just know it changed me. You see, I was the twelve-year-old boy who hung the sock on the fireplace. I've been trying to make people experience that same Christmas wonder ever since."

Jack and Joe smiled, but Katie still looked distant, distracted. So he tried another story, the story of the little girl who was deaf.

He recalled how dressed up she was when she came to see him. She had a red ribbon in her long black hair. She wore black patent leather shoes and white tights, and her red-and-green dress showed through her open black winter coat. Most of all, he told them how hesitant she was as she approached him.

"She looked at me for a long time before she sat in my lap," Santa said. "Then she used sign language to wish me 'Merry Christmas.' For a moment, she had this doubt in her eyes, like she wondered if I knew what she was doing. That's when I returned her 'Merry Christmas' in sign language, too. Her face glowed. She leaned against me and gave me this great big hug. Then she ran to her mom. Before she got there, she turned around and ran back to me. She used sign language again: 'I'd like a puppy for Christmas, if you have an extra one.' I signed back to her about the puppy, so the mother could see what she had asked for. The mother nodded yes so I told the girl I'd try my best. She gave me another big hug and ran to her mom, telling her that Santa had understood her. The little girl waved to me as they walked away. I saw her mother wiping away tears."

The story touched Katie. Still, she looked sad as she peered up at the man in the Santa suit and said, "You must love this time of year."

"Most of the time," he said. "But you also get to see some things that break your heart."

"What do you mean?" Jack asked.

Santa almost began the story about the six-year-old boy that he visited in this same hospital a few weeks ago. But when he looked at Katie, he still saw how vulnerable she was. He knew it wasn't the story she needed to hear at this time, in this place, so he shared a different one. He told them about one of the Christmas Eves when he and the people who help him loaded up food, clothes, toys, and those Charlie Brown Christmas trees that no one else wanted.

"I have helpers and we started going through poor neighborhoods about ten years ago," he said. "We searched for homes that didn't have a Christmas tree that we could see through the front window. After a few hours, we were down to one tree. I went up to this one house and knocked on the door. No one was home. So I peeked through the window. I couldn't believe how little they had in the living room. Just a beat-up sofa and a couple of chairs that looked in even worse shape. There was also a folding table with four metal chairs around it.

"We had just turned to leave when a woman came walking up the path with three small kids. The smallest child, a boy, just looked up at me in awe. His older brother and sister shouted, 'It's Santa! It's Santa!' They gave me hugs. And when their mother invited us inside, the three kids just kept talking and talking about what they wanted for Christmas. We gave them everything we had left on the truck. The next morning, we came back and gave the kids a few of the gifts they had told me about. Some of my helpers even brought extra furniture from their own homes."

"What a great story," Jack said, winking at Santa.

"You haven't heard my favorite one yet," Santa said.

"What's that?" Joe asked.

"It's about a girl at Christmas," Santa said. "My daughter."

"Tell us," Katie said.

Even though he had mentioned it, he wasn't sure he wanted to share the story. Every time he did, it always brought back so many emotions for him. Yet when he saw the expectant look on Katie's face, he knew he couldn't stop. He could tell that his stories had briefly distracted her from worrying about the baby.

"As everyone knows, Christmas Eve and Christmas morning are the busiest times for Santa," he said. "Everyone wants you to come to their homes or their parties to make Christmas special for their children. And some people will pay you a lot of money so they can have that extra touch. So I was always busy from about four o'clock in the afternoon on Christmas Eve to four o'clock in the afternoon on Christmas Day. That meant my wife and daughter opened presents on Christmas morning while I was working. We had to wait until late Christmas Day before I could celebrate with them. And a lot of times I was so worn out I fell asleep as soon as I sat down in the chair in front of our tree.

"One year on Christmas Eve, when my daughter was eleven, she told me she wanted me to stay home with her. She said she didn't care about all the other kids. She just wanted her daddy to be with her. I tried to explain to her how others counted on me. She listened and said, 'You're right, Daddy.' She even kissed me and said, 'Merry Christmas.' But I still saw the hurt in her eyes.

"On that Christmas morning, my daughter and my wife came down the stairs like they always had. But my wife later told me that my daughter said she didn't want to open her presents. Instead, she just curled up on the couch, hugging her stuffed toy penguin. She kept looking toward the front door.

"At that moment, I was at the house of a three-year-old boy and his parents. I was scheduled to be there for an hour. But as soon as I walked in the door and toward the boy, he started screaming and ran into his mother's arms. The parents tried to get the boy to warm up to me but he just kept crying and screaming. A minute later, the father thanked me and told me it wasn't going to work this year.

"Since I was in the neighborhood, I decided to go home. When I walked in the door, my daughter ran to me and hugged me. It was like her greatest Christmas wish had come true."

Fighting back the tears, he continued: "I wish I could say I had heard my daughter's wish and had done everything I could to make it happen. But I didn't. I was just lucky. Still, after that, I spent all my Christmas Eves and Christmas Days at home until she got married and moved away. Now, I'm the one who misses her at Christmas. You remind me of her, Katie. She's about your age."

Katie smiled and asked, "Where does she live now?"

"On the other side of the country, California," he said. "Every other year, I spend Christmas with her and her family. This year, they'll be coming here. We'll celebrate together this weekend."

Just around the corner from where the group sat, Anne Nelson leaned against the wall listening. She arrived there moments earlier, wanting to give an update about the baby. Yet when she heard the man in the Santa suit sharing the story about his daughter, she decided to wait until he finished. She walked around the corner just as Santa asked the cab driver, "What about you? You drive a cab on Christmas. You must have some stories."

"There's one," Jack said.

Before he could start, they saw the nurse.

⋆ Eight ⋆

Katie looked to the nurse with hope and fear in her eyes. Anne knew that look well from twenty-three years of caring for patients. Yet all her experience had never made it easier for her to deliver bad news to the families and friends of the people who came to the hospital for help. She once told her husband, "I have the best job in the world when a child gets to go home. Nothing matches the looks of parents when they know their child is going to live. But it's the worst job when a child dies. First, you lose the child. Then you watch a part of the parents die."

Anne wished she could give Katie and the three men the kind of news that would fill them with joy. But she couldn't. She could only give them hope, even if it was slim.

"I just want to let you know what's happening with the baby," she said as the four of them leaned forward in their chairs. "We were able to get him breathing again but then the doctor discovered the baby has a heart murmur. Fortunately, our best children's heart surgeon was in the hospital at the same time this morning, checking on a patient. He was called in to look at the baby.

"When he examined the baby, he decided the child needed emergency surgery. His surgery staff is on the way to the hospital right now. Once they begin the operation, which will be soon, it should last three to four hours. I'll try to let you know what's happening as soon as I can. Do you have any questions?"

"How good is this heart surgeon?" Joe asked.

"He's one of the best in the country for this kind of operation," Anne said. "But you should also know it's a delicate and serious procedure, especially with a baby involved."

"What are the chances of the baby surviving?" Katie asked, wrapping her arms around herself tightly.

"We're not sure," Anne said. "I just know that if it wasn't for you finding him and bringing him here as soon as you did, he never would have had this chance."

When they exhausted their questions, Joe said, "Thanks for taking the time to talk to us."

"You're welcome," Anne said. "I'll be back when there's more to tell you."

Before she left the waiting room, the nurse put her hand on Katie's shoulder, touching the worn, brown clothing of Mary that she still wore. Anne whispered to Katie, "Have faith."

The nurse told herself the same thing when she walked away. She remembered the anguished look on Dr. Lanzinger's face when he examined the baby in the emergency room. She remembered him telling her and the young doctor, "I've never heard a murmur so loud before in a baby. There's no doubt he has a hole in his heart. If we don't operate soon, I'm afraid he'll die. I'll have to call people in. Can you help me, Anne?"

"Any way I can," she said.

✳

Inside the hospital chapel, Jack knelt, slumping against the brown cushion behind him in the pew. He finished yet another prayer and looked to the front of the chapel where Katie and Joe had their heads bowed. They almost mirrored the poses of Mary and Joseph in the small Nativity scene at the foot of the chapel's altar. Turning to his left, Jack saw Santa praying, too, his red-and-white hat behind him on the oak bench. Jack looked at his gold watch. Two hours had passed since they were told the baby's surgery had started.

For Jack, three days had passed since he sat in this same hospital chapel, praying for himself. The chapel was the first place he came after his meeting with a doctor who specializes in prostate cancer. Tests results showed Jack had the disease. His operation was scheduled for next Tuesday.

When Jack entered the hospital three days ago, he came alone. He still hadn't told anyone about the cancer or the need for surgery. He had no relatives, and even though he had always tried to treat his employees like family, he didn't tell any of his drivers or his staff. He didn't want to burden them with the news just before Christmas.

Joe rose from the pew in front of the chapel and walked toward Jack and Santa.

"Katie wants to head back to the waiting room to see if there is any news about the baby," Joe whispered to the two men. "We can meet you there if you'd like to stay here for now. Or maybe you want to get something to eat in the cafeteria."

"No, we'll come with you," Jack whispered.

Santa nodded his head, too.

The four of them rode an elevator to a private waiting area near the operating room. They had been brought there shortly after Anne had told them the baby was going into surgery. Anne knew the place was more private and comfortable than the waiting area for the emergency room so she sent an orderly to the emergency room to bring them there.

"What do they look like?" the orderly asked Anne.

"You can't miss them," she said with a smile. "There's a guy in a Santa suit and he's with a young couple dressed like Mary and Joseph. There's also a cab driver with them who looks like he just stepped off the boat from Ireland."

When the orderly first brought them to the room, Katie asked him if he could also give them directions to the chapel. They had been there most of the past two hours.

Inside the waiting room again, Katie picked up a *People* magazine and put it down in the same motion. Joe leaned forward in his chair, putting his hands on both sides of his light-brown beard. He then raked his hands through his hair. Santa and Jack both looked at the husband and wife. Then they glanced at each other.

"When we were in the emergency room, you said you had a story about being a cabbie on Christmas," Santa said to Jack. "What's the story?"

"It's a long one," Jack said. "I'm not sure it's the right time for it."

"I'd like to hear it," Katie said, looking up at him.

Just as her vulnerability had made Jack stop his cab in the street for her, so it made him sit down and start his story.

"Okay," Jack told her. "If you haven't noticed from my brogue, I was born and grew up in Ireland. I was an orphan. When I was fifteen, I got a job on a cargo ship heading to America. It was 1951. I got all the worst jobs on the ship. I had nothing and no one back at home so I decided I wasn't going back. I snuck off the ship when it docked. It didn't matter that I didn't know anyone here.

"That first night, I walked the streets looking for a place to stay. Found one in a park shelter. It was cold, but at least it kept me dry from the rain that night. The next morning, I hit the streets again and found a small restaurant called O'Malley's. Figured a place with a name like that would be willing to help an Irish kid just off the boat. Figured wrong. Even with a map of Ireland on the wall, the owner wanted to see my money first. When it wasn't American money, he told me to get lost. Didn't even want to listen when I told him I was born and grew up in Ireland. 'You and thousands of other people in this city,' he said, waving me toward the door. But there was another guy in the restaurant eating. Offered me a seat and half of a fried egg sandwich with ketchup. Said his name was Sean Murphy. Told O'Malley to bring me some more food—eggs, potatoes, ham, the works. Wanted to know the rest of my story. When I finished, he said he could use some clean-up help at the cab company he owned. Wanted to know if I could use a job. Took me less than a second to answer.

"Mr. Murphy was one of those big, ruddy-faced guys. The people in the cab company said he had an easy smile and a great sense of humor, too. But that was before his son, Tim, was drafted to fight in the Korean War. Tim was just a few years older than me. He was the Murphys' only kid. Sometimes I thought Mr. Murphy regarded me as his on-loan son. While he looked out for me, he hoped God would look out for his son. Mrs. Murphy had a different approach. She prayed for her son constantly and didn't have any interest in me. When Mr. Murphy asked her if I could stay with them for a while, she said no. I didn't mind. I was used to being by myself. Besides, he gave me a job, found me a place to stay, and always asked how I was doing. I was living better than I ever had.

"The more work I did, the more responsibility he gave me. He even said yes when I asked him to show me how to drive one of the cabs. I was a quick learner. That proved to be good in the Christmas of 1952. The Murphys were hoping their son might be able to come home for Christmas that year. But he couldn't. Still, Mr. Murphy decided to give free cab rides to any serviceman coming home that Christmas. He said it was his small way of saying thanks for all the sacrifices they were making.

"When one of the drivers got loaded early Christmas Eve, Mr. Murphy asked if I could drive that cab instead. It was the chance I had waited for. I was at the train station when these two guys in Army uniforms got into the cab. One lived in the city. The other lived west of it.

In a small town. You shoulda heard these guys. They couldn't believe they were heading home for Christmas. They were like kids on Christmas morning. Except when they talked for a short time about the war. Then they didn't look or sound like kids anymore.

"When I dropped off the city guy, he wished us both 'Merry Christmas' and asked me to tell Mr. Murphy the same. 'Now, it's my turn,' said the other guy. I still remember his name. Will Ferguson. His home was about twenty miles away. As we headed west, sleet began to fall, then freezing rain. Before long, cars and trucks were sliding off the slick roads. I thought about stopping or turning back. I had never driven in those conditions before. But in the back of my mind, I kept hearing Mr. Murphy. Talking about the sacrifices the soldiers and sailors were making for us. And how we had to make sacrifices for them. I figured he would want me to do everything I could do to get this guy home. So I kept driving on, slower and slower. Out in the country, the roads got narrow and deserted. It was so dark out there, except for the lights from a farmhouse every half-mile or so. At one point, Will said, 'Thanks for doing this. It's just about two miles from here.' That's when I misjudged a curve, tried to brake, and lost control of the cab. We ended up in a ditch.

"We tried to push it out but we couldn't. Will opened the door to the cab, pulled out his duffel bag, and started walking up the hill. I couldn't believe it. He was going to leave me, I said to myself. After all I had tried to do for him. But when he got to the top of the hill, he turned around and said, 'Come on. We'll walk the last couple of miles. We'll get some help tomorrow to pull the cab out.' So we walked for what seemed like forever, sliding and slipping on the ice. All while a wicked wind whipped against us. We were out there at least two hours. I was freezing and tired but none of it seemed to matter to him. He just kept walking. It was like he was being pulled by something or someone. Someone who waited for him. Someone he would cross a world to see. It was a feeling I'd never known. I just followed along. Finally, we reached his house. It was like a beacon. Nearly every light was on inside. It was two stories tall, light-blue and it had a wrap-around, white porch. He just stood there, looking at the house for the longest time. Then he ran up the steps and knocked on the front door. I was just a few steps behind him. When the door opened, it was his mother. She put her hands to her face. She yelled to her husband and began crying.

"She wrapped her arms around her son. She didn't let go of him for the longest time. Then it was his father bear-hugging him. And his younger brothers and sisters. I just watched in awe. In envy, too.

"After his hero's welcome, Will turned and introduced me to everyone. They couldn't thank me enough for helping him get home. His mother hugged me and kissed my cheek. They invited me to stay the night. They told me they would help me with the cab in the morning. They also let me use their phone to call Mr. Murphy. He told me not to worry about the cab. That he was just glad I was fine and I'd helped the guy get home. But there seemed to be a sadness in his voice, too. I guess he was thinking about his own son.

"That night, we all sat down at the kitchen table. The mother kept cooking and placing food before the two of us. A ham. Bread. A chocolate cake. Milk. A cherry pie. Coffee. His family told him the news of the town, the news of the family. His youngest brother wanted to show him his toy army helmet. His little sister wanted to give him the Christmas present she made for him. And people kept getting up from their chairs to touch him and hug him. I had never seen anything like it. It lasted until two in the morning. It was the same way five hours later when everyone got up to celebrate Christmas. I watched the younger kids rip open the two presents they each received for Christmas. And I couldn't believe it when the youngest sister handed me a gift, too. A card. In crayon. She thanked me for bringing her brother home. Through it all, I kept sneaking looks at the parents. They kept looking from their oldest son to their other children. And they both had these huge smiles on their faces.

"I stayed through breakfast. More relatives and friends flooded through the front door. More hugs and handshakes all around. Then Will and his father helped me get the cab out of the ditch. The father drove the tractor there while Will took me in a pickup truck. They hooked a chain from the tractor to the cab. They got it back on the road in seconds.

"Before I drove away, Will and his father thanked me again for making it their best Christmas ever. I felt the same way, but I wasn't sure they would have understood if I said that.

"So that's my Christmas story."

"It's wonderful," Katie said.

Jack nodded and smiled.

"What ever happened to Mr. Murphy's son?" Joe asked.

"I was hoping no one would ask," Jack said. "It's the hard part of the story. Tim was killed in action in January of 1953. Less than a month after I gave those two guys a ride home on Christmas. Mrs. Murphy fell apart. Mr. Murphy was crushed."

Jack sighed as he looked down at the floor.

"Even after his son died, Mr. Murphy looked out for me," Jack said, almost in a whisper. "I tried to do the same for him and Mrs. Murphy as I got older. But there was always a sadness there. I ran the cab company for him the last five years of his life. When he died, he left the company to me. As a tribute to him, I never charge passengers in my cab on Christmas Eve and Christmas Day."

★

As Jack finished his story, a young nurse with short blonde hair stopped by the waiting room to see if they needed anything.

"Is there any news about the baby?" Katie asked.

"Not yet," the nurse said. "We're hoping to hear something soon but it's hard to say. Sometimes, you never know everything that's involved until you can see inside the patient."

In the operating room, Dr. Lanzinger leaned over the baby. More than two and a half hours had passed since he first cut an incision in the child's chest to reach his heart. He had expected to find trouble, but this situation was worse than he had thought. The hole in the baby's heart was bigger than any he had ever seen in an infant. Complicating his condition, the child had been born with its major vessels in the places opposite of where they should be, affecting the flow of blood to the heart.

Dr. Lanzinger knew the next twenty minutes of the operation would be critical. Just as he had always done at these times, he said a short prayer that he and his staff would be able to do what needed to be done. Finishing the prayer, he looked at Anne Nelson on the other side of the table. Dr. Lanzinger requested Anne's help when one of his regular team members couldn't make it into the hospital because freezing rain had hit her area of the city.

"This is where it gets tricky," Lanzinger told Anne. "Are you ready?"

"I'm a little nervous," Anne said.

"So am I," the doctor said.

✴ NINE ✴

Stopped at a red light, Detective Piersall looked at the brown blanket next to him on the front seat. Touching its frayed edges, he wondered how the baby was doing in surgery. He also wondered about the child's mother. Who was she? Where was she? Why would she abandon her baby?

The detective wasn't any closer to answering those questions since getting the report of the abandoned baby. He had visited the emergency rooms of the three other hospitals in the city. The admissions clerks in all three emergency rooms told him that no one had arrived seeking treatment for injuries from childbirth.

"Here's my card," Piersall told the clerks. "Call me right away if someone does."

Earlier in the day, he had visited Our Mother of Sorrows Church where the baby was found. He had searched the stable scene for any other clues besides the brown blanket, but hadn't found anything. The falling snow had covered the footprints that Katie had seen.

A few minutes ago, Piersall had made a return trip to the church to talk to Father Angelos. The priest had been busy earlier celebrating three Masses. Piersall asked Father Angelos if he knew of anyone in the parish who was pregnant.

"Two that I know of," the priest said as he took off his vestments and relaxed in a chair. "I saw them both receive Communion at the last Mass and both were still very much pregnant."

Now, as the light turned green, Piersall headed straight through the intersection. The detective drove slower than usual because the snow continued to fall, making the roads slick. Seconds later, he cursed himself for not driving even more cautiously. A small boy pulling a wooden sled stepped into the street from between two parked cars. Piersall jammed on the horn and the brakes, feeling the car beginning to skid immediately. Turning toward the sound, the boy in the blue coat and a blue-and-gold stocking cap froze in the middle of the street.

Piersall saw the shock in the child's eyes first, then the fear. He felt the car's tires trying to grip the road. He pulled back on the steering wheel, desperately trying anything to will the car from hitting the boy. Still, the car kept sliding toward the child. Then he saw the boy fall and disappear from his view as the car finally stopped.

Opening the driver's door, the detective rushed toward the boy. He found him kneeling in the slushy snow of the street. The car's silver front bumper was just two inches from the boy's body.

"Are you okay?" the detective asked as he knelt by the boy.

"Yeah…I think so," the boy said, breathing hard. "The car…didn't hit me."

After catching his breath, the boy flashed a nervous smile and said, "It worked."

"What worked?" Piersall asked.

"Kneeling," the boy said. "Our Sunday School teacher told us that when we get in trouble, we should kneel and say a prayer and God will take care of us. That's what I did when I didn't think the car was going to stop."

Piersall didn't know what to say. His faith had long ago been shaken by all the horror he had seen in his job. Besides, he was nearly certain the Sunday School teacher never meant her advice to be used when a car was heading right at you. But none of that mattered at that moment, he figured. The detective helped the boy to his feet and asked, "What's your name?"

"C.J. Johnson," the boy said as he wiped the snow from the knees of his pants.

"My name is Detective Piersall. I'm with the police department," he said, showing his badge.

"How old are you, C.J.?"

"Eight. And three-quarters. I turn nine in March."

"Where do you live?"

"Right around the corner, on Harwood."

"Are your parents home? I should take you there and tell them what happened."

"My mom's working at the nursing home today. I was going there when…Oh, God, she'll kill me. She always tells me to cross at the light. You don't have to tell her, do you?"

"We'll see," Piersall said. "What about your father?"

"He doesn't live with us anymore," the boy said, looking away from the detective's stare.

"My sled," C.J. said as a look of panic crossed his face. "Is it okay?"

The detective retrieved the sled from under the car. Then he checked the runners and the steering mechanism. Like the sled, they were old but they still seemed straight and functional.

"It looks like everything works," Piersall said. C.J. sighed in relief.

Still holding the sled, Piersall saw the faded Flexible Flyer logo. It reminded him of a Christmas long ago when his parents gave him the same kind of sled as a present. He was six then, and his father took him and his little sister sledding on a nearby hill. He knew there was still a picture of the three of them on the sled: his dad on the bottom, he on top of his dad, and his sister on top of him. His mother had taken the photo, capturing the three of them smiling and laughing. For the next few years, his family had also used the sled when they went to buy a Christmas tree at a neighborhood lot strung with white lights. Heading to the lot, his father pulled him and his sister on the sled. On the way home, his dad carried the middle of the tree and he carried the back while his mom walked alongside, pulling his sister on the sled. He also recalled how the four of them always sang Christmas carols on those trips. He remembered those moments as a magical time in his life. Yet instead of smiling at the thought, he looked sad.

Then he noticed C.J. on his knees again, in the slush. The boy searched through a white plastic bag, as if he was trying to determine that its contents were still intact.

"What's that?" the detective asked.

"A bag of gifts," C.J. said. "I had it on the sled before. . ."

He reached in the direction toward a parked red car, picking up a small doll with brown curly hair from the black-streaked snow. After he brushed snow from the doll's blue dress, he looked around again, finally focusing on something under the detective's car.

"Could you get that for me?" C.J. asked, pointing under the car.

Piersall leaned the sled against the side of the car. He knelt on one knee, holding onto the front bumper with his left hand as he looked under the car. Seeing a baseball in the middle of the two front tires, he reached and grabbed it.

"Is this one of your gifts?" Piersall asked C.J., holding the baseball toward him.

"It's for someone at the nursing home," C.J. said, taking the ball. "I go there when my mom's working sometimes. Some of the old people like to talk to me. About when they were kids. Mr. Walters likes baseball. Jackie Robinson was his favorite player."

Piersall smiled. "My dad loved baseball," he said. "He taught me the game." The detective looked away. "But that was a long time ago." Piersall paused. "Who's the doll for?" he asked.

"A lady named Mrs. Kennedy. She told me her favorite Christmas was the year she got her first doll."

"What else you got in that bag?"

"A yo-yo. A plane. A ballerina. And some other things I thought would remind them of being a kid. I already had most of the stuff at home. Except for the doll and the ballerina. I got those at the dollar store. It's all good stuff. Not the underwear and socks other people give them. I hate getting underwear and socks for Christmas. I bet they do, too."

Piersall laughed.

"You're something else, C.J.," the detective said. "Hop in the car and I'll drive you over to the nursing home. It's the one on Paxson, right?"

"Yeah, that's it. How did you know?" C.J. said. Before the detective could answer, C.J. asked another question, "What about my sled?"

"I'll put it in the trunk," Piersall said.

When they were both inside the car, the detective said, "That's a good sled you have. I had one just like it when I was a kid."

"My grandmother said it was my father's when he was a boy," C.J. said, slumping back into the seat.

The detective didn't know how to respond. Instead, he asked, "Are there any good places for sledding around here?"

"There's a hill in a park, just a couple of blocks from here," C.J. said. "I've heard some of the kids in the neighborhood talk about how great it is. My mom said she's going to take me there after work sometime but she's always tired when she gets done."

"What time does she get off?" Piersall asked as he made a right turn.

"Two-thirty," the boy said as the car passed a row of boarded-up houses. "We're going home and having Christmas when she gets done."

"You haven't had Christmas yet?"

"No. Mom went to work at six. My grandmother said we had to wait for my mom to get home before we celebrate. It's making me crazy. What did you get?"

"What do you mean?"

"For Christmas. What did your kids and your wife get you?"

"I don't have any kids. And I'm not married anymore."

"Why not?"

"My ex-wife said I paid more attention to my job than her. So she left."

"My father left, too," C.J. said, looking out the passenger window. "I was two. That's what my mom said. I don't remember him, but I think about him a lot."

"I think about my dad, too," Piersall said.

"What do you think about?" C.J. asked, looking at the detective's face.

"Well, Christmas was his favorite time of year," Piersall said. He braked cautiously as a traffic light turned yellow. "We'd put up our tree on Christmas Eve and decorate it. And every year, no matter how bad the tree was, he'd say it was the best one we ever had, because we were all around it together. He also loved when it snowed. Whenever it did, he'd take me and my sister sledding. We'd be out there for hours."

C.J. grew quiet. He didn't say anything for a long time until he saw a green sign with white letters, for Sellers Park.

"That's where it is," C.J. said, pointing to the sign.

"What?" Piersall asked.

"The hill. The one all the kids talk about," the boy said. "Hey, will you take me there?"

"Sorry. I can't. I really need to check something out, right after I drop you off at the nursing home."

"Please? Just one time. It's Christmas," the boy said as he turned toward the detective, his eyes begging.

When he looked back on that moment later, Piersall tried to analyze what made him change his mind. Maybe it was because he came so close to hitting the boy with his car. Or maybe it had something to do with thinking about his own dad and all the things he did for him and his sister, and how C.J. couldn't even remember his father. And maybe it was connected to what his ex-wife said right after she told him she wanted a divorce. The words still haunted him.

"Your mind is always on a case instead of the person right in front of you," she told him.

Whatever the reason, Piersall made a right turn into the park and stopped the car by the top of the hill. C.J. sat there, stunned.

"Come on," Piersall said as he opened the driver's door. "I figure you have time for one ride before I have to get back to work and get you to the nursing home."

C.J. exploded from the car.

Getting the sled from the trunk, Piersall handed it to C.J. Beaming, the boy ran to the top of the hill, pulling the sled behind him. He couldn't wait to jump on the sled and fly down the snowy hill. Yet C.J. stopped when he looked down at the long slope, the tall trees on either side of it, and the creek at the bottom of the hill. Piersall noticed the boy's expression had changed from anticipation to fear.

C.J. turned and looked up at Piersall. "You wanna ride, too?" the boy asked.

Piersall scanned the hill crowded with parents and children. He thought about how he was dressed in his gray coat, a dark blue suit, and a silver tie. He was certain that no one had ever been more inappropriately dressed for a sledding hill.

"Sure," Piersall finally said, even though he hadn't been on a sled in about 20 years.

While Piersall held it, C.J. sat on the front half of the sled. The detective slid onto the back half, maneuvering his feet into position to control the steering bar. As he held the sled's rope with his right hand, Piersall used his left to push against the snow. Slowly, the sled crested over the hill, picking up speed as they began hurtling down the slope. The pace stunned them, excited them, leaving them laughing and screaming.

"Oh, my God," Piersall whispered as they approached a bump. "Hold on!"

Reaching back, C.J. clung to Piersall's coat just before they hit the bump. They hung in the air for what seemed like forever, both of them gasping. When the sled slammed into the earth again, the snow flew up and kicked back into their faces. It blinded C.J. for a moment. Wiping the snow from his eyes, the boy saw they were headed straight for a bank of trees near the creek. Piersall saw the trees, too. He also felt C.J. lean back into him. As Piersall shifted his weight to the left, the detective pushed his right foot into the right side of the sled's steering bar. The maneuver sent them passing safely in front of the trees before they came to a stop.

C.J. hopped from the sled and said, "That was awesome! What a ride!" He began to dance across the snow.

Piersall sat on the sled and smiled at the show.

When C.J. finished dancing, Piersall rose to his feet, grabbed the sled's rope, and walked toward the boy.

"That was a cool last turn you made," C.J. said, smiling.

"I guess you never forget how to do some things," Piersall said.

"Thanks for the ride," C.J. said as he clutched the sled's rope, too.

The two sons began to walk up the hill, pulling the sled together.

✴ TEN ✴

In the waiting room, Jack turned to Katie and Joe.

"What about you, Joe and Katie?" he asked. "Before today, were there any Christmases that stood out to you?"

Joe wished the question had never been asked. He wondered if Katie would answer it.

Katie didn't say anything for a long time. She even covered her face with her hands for a while. Finally, she sighed and said, "Last year."

The answer made Joe cringe.

Like a shadow, sorrow crossed Katie's face. She looked at Santa and said, "As Santa, you've probably known plenty of children who tell you their Christmas and their life will be perfect if you can bring them that one special gift they've always wanted."

Santa nodded.

"I had that same feeling a year ago when I woke up on Christmas morning," Katie said. "Joe was by my side. I was pregnant with our first child. It was just exactly as Mrs. Williams had told us. When she first asked us to play Mary and Joseph, she jokingly warned us that every Mary who had played the part before had been pregnant when she stepped into the stable. That hadn't happened to us for the first several years but then last year it did. We couldn't have been more thrilled. After all those years of trying to have a baby, we were finally going to have one.

"Sitting in that stable last Christmas, I kept thinking about Mary. About her example as a mother. And all the sacrifices she made for Jesus. And I couldn't wait to do that for my child. I wanted to give life. I wanted to care for him or her with my whole heart and soul. When I was in that stable last year, I felt I was living my own Christmas miracle. I had never been closer to God."

She paused. "By Christmas night, I had lost the baby, here in this hospital. I had a miscarriage."

She stopped talking and put down her head. The three men saw her tears falling to the floor.

Joe put his arm around her shoulder and whispered, "It's okay, Katie. It's okay." Tears fell from his eyes, too.

"It started when I felt this deep pain in my abdomen," Katie said as she lifted her head and wiped her tears. "Then I began bleeding. I shouted for Joe and he came running up the stairs. I told him something was wrong with the baby, we had to get to the hospital. All the time we were driving there, I kept thinking this couldn't be happening. Not after all our years of waiting. Not on Christmas. I kept praying, 'God, please let the baby be alive. Please. I'll do anything.'

"When we got to the emergency room, they rushed us right in. 'Do something!' I begged them."

She paused before she whispered, "But it was too late."

Joe lowered his head.

Katie continued in the soft whisper that made Jack and Santa lean forward to hear.

"I had carried our son for more than four months, the best four months of my life," she said. "All during that time, I had dreamed of holding my baby in my arms. That's all I wanted to do. Hold my baby."

Katie started to cry again.

"It devastated me," she said through the tears. "When we got home from the hospital, I just crawled into bed and stayed there. I just felt empty. For months, I cried every time I saw a baby. And the pain hasn't really gone away. Joe has been trying to tell me for a year now that God has a plan for us, that everything will work out according to that plan."

She looked at Joe. "He has faith. I've lost mine. I didn't want to be part of the Living Nativity again this year but Joe thought it would be good for us. Now here we are again this Christmas, in this hospital, with another baby dying. And I'm wondering what the hell is wrong with God."

Her body shook. She sobbed loudly. Her tears flowed. Through it all, Joe held her.

✳ ELEVEN ✳

In a corner of the operating room, Anne slumped against a table. Across the room, Dr. Lanzinger collapsed into a chair and ran his hands through his white hair. Everyone else on Lanzinger's team showed similar signs of emotional exhaustion. Yet both the doctor and the nurse knew they had one more task to complete. As they walked to the waiting room, Anne finally had the opportunity to tell the doctor how the baby arrived at the hospital. She also told him about the group of people he would soon meet.

Jack and Santa rose from their chairs when the doctor and nurse entered the waiting room. Joe put his arm around Katie. All four braced themselves for what they were about to hear.

"I have good news," the doctor said. "We were able to fix the baby's heart."

Santa pumped his fist in the air. Jack shouted, "Yes!" Katie and Joe hugged each other. Then everyone started hugging everyone else. Jack even gave Lanzinger a hug.

"I just want to tell you a couple more things," the doctor said. "The baby will be in the intensive care unit for a while. We need to keep an eye on him and build up his strength as much as we can. The other thing I want to say is, 'Thank you.' Anne told me what each of you did for this child. You should all be proud of yourselves. Now if you'll excuse me, I'm a few hours late for Christmas with my grandkids. If you have any questions, I think Anne will be able to answer them."

"Thanks again, Doctor," Joe said as Lanzinger left.

"Can we see him?" Katie asked Anne.

"Not right now," the nurse said. "He needs his rest. Maybe tomorrow. We have a program at the hospital where people can volunteer to come in to hold and rock babies when their parents can't. If you're interested, I can get you some information."

"I'd love that," Katie said.

"Let's go somewhere and celebrate," Jack said.

"Before you do, I wonder if I could have your help for a little while, Santa?" Anne asked.

"Sure," Santa said.

"I need to go to the chapel," Katie said. "I need to say thank you this time."

"Let's meet in the cafeteria in an hour," Jack said.

Everyone agreed.

✳ TWELVE ✳

In the nursing home's snow-covered parking lot, Detective Piersall opened the trunk to his car and pulled out C.J.'s sled.

"I'll take it inside for you. You already have your hands full," Piersall said, nodding toward the white bag of gifts the boy held.

When they were inside the front doors of the nursing home, C.J. told Piersall he could put the sled in the corner near a large potted plant.

"That's where I always leave my stuff," the boy said. "Anything there, they know it's mine." Then he looked up at the detective and said, "Thanks again, Mister. That was so much fun."

"Yeah, I had a good time, too," Piersall said.

"Well, I better get going," C.J. said. "I have to deliver these gifts before my mom's shift ends."

"Merry Christmas, C.J."

C.J. walked toward Piersall, gave him a hug and said, "Merry Christmas."

Seconds later, Piersall watched the boy walk down the hall and disappear into the second room on the right. The detective headed toward the front door but halfway there, he stopped and reversed his steps, stopping by an elevator. He rode it to the third floor. Getting off, Piersall walked down a hall toward the nursing home's Alzheimer's unit. After checking in at the unit's security desk, he turned down another hall. The detective finally stopped at a door that had a "Season's Greetings" sign on it. Opening the door slightly, he peeked inside. Piersall could see his father sleeping peacefully on the bed.

Entering the room, the detective stepped into his family's past. His mother and his sister visited regularly, and nearly every time they came, they seemed to bring a new photo. The pictures covered every part of the room. From the dresser, he picked up a picture of the four of them on the beach when he and his sister were kids. Putting it back, he placed it near a shot of his sister and dad at a father-daughter dance, right next to a picture of his parents celebrating their twenty-fifth wedding anniversary, and a photo of him and his father smiling at his graduation from the police academy.

He once asked his mother if she was hoping all the photos would lead to a miraculous recovery of his father's memory.

"Wouldn't that be wonderful," his mother said, lost for a moment in that dream. "But that's not why I do it. I just want your father to be surrounded by us at all times, especially when we're not here."

Piersall knew his mother and sister had kept the faith of being there for his father. They had come regularly to visit. He hadn't. It pained him to see his father as a shell of the man he once was. It pained him even more that his father so seldom recognized any of them. Even on his infrequent visits, Piersall would leave as quickly as he could.

Walking across the room, Piersall sat in the green chair next to his father's bed. He could hear his father snoring softly as he put his hand on top of his father's hand. Just then, his cell phone began vibrating. Piersall pulled the phone from his pocket and immediately recognized that the number displayed was from the emergency room of the hospital where the abandoned baby was in surgery.

Just before he started to press the button to take the call, he noticed the framed photo of his father, his sister, and him on the sled from that Christmas Day long ago. It was right on the wall where he knew it would be. As he let the phone call flow into his voice mail, he promised himself that he would return the call in a minute. For now, he looked at the photo again and tightened his hold on his father's hand.

⋆ THIRTEEN ⋆

Anne led Santa onto the elevator heading toward the pediatric intensive care unit.

"I was hoping you could make a special visit to a child for me," Anne said.

"That's fine," Santa said. "That's what I do on Christmas."

"Her name is Sally. She's six years old. She's one of Dr. Lanzinger's patients, too. He performed heart transplant surgery on her earlier this month. She's scheduled to go home in a few days but she's been depressed ever since the transplant. She keeps thinking about the little boy who had to die so she could get a heart."

"Six?" Santa said. "In early December I got an emergency phone call from a mother and father telling me it didn't look like their six-year-old son would live until Christmas. They wanted to know if I could visit their son earlier. Bobby was in this hospital. When I came into his room, he just had this look of joy when he saw me. It broke my heart when I checked the next day and learned Bobby had died. I wonder if he's the same boy whose heart Sally has."

Anne looked at him, stunned. Finally, she said, "That's him. He was one of my patients. A beautiful boy. I was crushed when he died." She paused as the elevator door opened. "So you were the Santa he talked about. He couldn't stop talking about your visit. He loved it."

They stepped off the elevator and walked down the hall toward Sally's room. When Sally saw Santa before her, she couldn't believe it. Her expression changed in seconds from surprise to joy.

"Merry Christmas, Sally," Santa said. He pointed to several gifts on her bed. "I see you've had a good Christmas so far."

"Thank you for the doll," Sally said with a smile. "It's just the one I wanted. I got some books, too. My mom and dad gave me them. They just went home to be with my little brother. But they're coming back."

"Good," Santa said. "How are you feeling today? I hear you have a new heart."

The joy suddenly disappeared from Sally's face.

"It's not mine," she said softly, casting her eyes toward the floor. "I feel bad I got it because another kid died."

Santa put his white-gloved hand on Sally's shoulder.

"Think of your new heart as a gift," Santa said. "When someone gives you a gift, they want you to enjoy it. The boy's family gave you this heart because they wanted you to have it. They wanted a part of their little boy to live, too. So you're giving them a gift, too, by using it. I just have one favor to ask of you, Sally."

"What's that?" the girl said, looking up at Santa.

"Do good things with your new heart," he said.

Sally smiled and reached up her hands to hug him.

Santa stayed with Sally for thirty minutes. During part of that time, he thought about Bobby as he looked at her. For another twenty minutes, he visited the other children on the unit who were too sick to go home. Even as they struggled, their spirits seemed to soar when they saw him, just knowing he had made a special trip for them. The visits had the same effect on him. He felt a peace inside himself when he left the last child's room and headed toward the elevator. He found Anne there, waiting to return to the emergency room for the rest of her shift.

"I've been wondering about all the people who just happened to be here today," Santa told Anne when they were inside the elevator. "Jack, Katie, Joe, Dr. Lanzinger. I've been wondering about you, too. You obviously have enough experience that you wouldn't have to work Christmas if you didn't want to."

She told him about wanting to see Sally. She also told him about her husband dying in October and how it was just too hard for her to be alone at home on this first Christmas without him.

"Jeff loved Christmas," she said. "The first year we were married, he surprised me by buying a live Christmas tree for us and planting it in the front yard. He decorated it with lights and put a star on the top of it. When he took me out to see it, he told me, 'The star will be our sign of hope every year, no matter what happens.' Every fifth anniversary, he planted another evergreen tree in the yard. Each Christmas we would decorate them with lights and a star. You should have seen it. From the smallest tree to the biggest one, the lights would lead up to the sky. Like a comet. It was so beautiful. We got so much joy out of it. But I just couldn't do it this year without him."

"I'm sorry," Santa said. "I wish I could do something for you."

"You have—by visiting Sally and the other children," she said. "Thank you."

The elevator opened at the level for the emergency room.

"Merry Christmas," Anne said.

"Merry Christmas, Anne."

After he watched her walk away, Santa pushed the elevator button for the cafeteria. Jack, Katie and Joe were already there, looking at a black-board menu that featured sliced turkey, ham, yams, mashed potatoes, green beans, apple pie, and cherry Jello with whipped cream. They each took a tray and headed down the line. At the cash register, Jack insisted on paying.

"None of my passengers ever pays on Christmas," he said.

"But I haven't been in your cab," Santa said.

"I'm giving you a ride home with Katie and Joe," Jack said. "So you will be my passenger on Christmas Day."

As Jack pulled his wallet from his pants, he didn't notice a small card fall from his pocket. Santa did. He picked it up. He was ready to return it to Jack, but then he looked at it and put the card in his own pocket.

Their dinner together was a celebration marked by joy, tears, smiles, and laughter. At one point, Jack sat back as the others relived the incred-ible day. He just took it all in, looking at their faces, savoring the moment and his new friends.

"By the way, Santa," Katie asked after a sip of hot tea, "what's your real name?"

"Whenever I wear this suit, I'm Santa," he said, winking.

"Of course," Katie said, smiling.

"What do you do for a life?" Santa asked her.

"I'm a teacher," she said. "I teach kindergarten."

"Little kids," Santa said, nodding. "I love the way they believe. They're the ones who keep me returning every year. They believe and they make me believe, too. It's a wonderful gift I get from them."

His eyes had a dreamy look.

"And how about you, Joe?" Santa asked.

"I own a business that cuts and trims trees," Joe said.

"Imagine that," Santa said, laughing. "A man named Joe who plays Joseph in a Live Nativity, and he works in the wood business. The next thing you'll tell me is that you do carpentry as a hobby."

"No, I play the piano," Joe said. "You should hear me play *Santa Claus Is Coming To Town*."

Everyone laughed.

After the meal, Jack insisted on driving everyone home. He even told Joe and Katie he would call a friend in the towing business to fix their flat tire and bring their car home for free. When Jack pulled in front of Katie and Joe's house, Katie hugged Santa and Jack one more time. She also told Jack, "None of this would have happened without you. Like I told you this morning, you're an angel."

"It's been my pleasure," Jack said, tipping his hat.

"Thank you for everything, both of you," Joe said to Jack and Santa.

"Never stop believing," Santa said.

"We won't, not after today," Katie said.

As the young couple walked toward their house, Joe slipped his right arm around Katie's shoulder.

Back in the cab, Jack said to Santa, "Some days you hate to see end."

"I feel that way every Christmas," Santa said. He reached into his pocket.

"By the way, Jack, when we were in the cafeteria, this card fell out of your pocket when you pulled out your wallet. It says here that you have an appointment for cancer surgery scheduled for next Tuesday."

"Yeah," Jack said, looking down. "It's my prostate. I'm getting old, I guess."

"I just want to let you know I'll be there with you at the hospital Tuesday," Santa said.

Jack looked up at Santa. "That would really help. Thank you. If there's ever anything I can do to return the favor, just let me know."

"As a matter of fact, there is right now," Santa said. "I have a couple of places I need to stop before I go home. If you have the time, I could use your help. There's one more gift I need to deliver for Christmas."

"Sure thing," Jack said.

"Come to think of it," Santa said, "we could use Joe and Katie's help, too. Let me see if they'd be willing to give us a hand."

Santa climbed out of the cab and started humming *O, Holy Night* as he walked toward Joe and Katie's front door.

★ FOURTEEN ★

Three hours later, the present had been wrapped, decorated and delivered. While Jack, Joe, and Katie marveled at the gift, Santa checked his watch and saw it was 7 p.m. At that same time, Anne Nelson ended her twelve-hour shift in the emergency room. She said "Merry Christmas" to the arriving nurses and headed toward the elevator. Just then, a clerk at the admissions desk called to her. Turning, Anne saw the clerk. She also noticed a man in a rumpled gray coat at the desk, looking in her direction. The nurse walked toward them.

"Anne, this is Detective Piersall," the clerk said. "He's investigating what happened to the baby who was abandoned."

"Hello, Nurse Nelson," the detective said, nodding toward Anne. "I got the good news earlier that everything went well in surgery. I was in the neighborhood and wanted to see if the baby was still doing fine."

"He is," Anne said. "I just called up to the intensive care unit a few minutes ago. The nurses said he was resting peacefully and his vital signs are stable."

"Good, great," Piersall said. "I haven't had any luck finding the mother yet but at least the kid is all right. That's what counts." Then he paused before adding, "I was wondering if I could see him?"

"I don't think it's a good time," Anne said. "He's had a traumatic day. Is it important for your investigation?"

Piersall wasn't sure he could explain to anyone why he wanted to see the baby. Still, he saw something in the nurse's face, especially her warm brown eyes, that made him try.

"It can wait," the detective said. "It's just that ever since I got the report about the baby...It's hard to explain. I've just met a lot of good people and had a lot of good things happen today. That's never the case when I work Christmas. And it all traces back to a baby I haven't seen."

"Let me call intensive care and see what they say," Anne said.

"No, it's okay," Piersall said, shaking his head. "He needs his rest. Just knowing he's still doing fine is enough for now. I'll stop by tomorrow and see if it's a better time. Besides, there's one more lead I need to check."

"Are you sure?"

The detective nodded. "Thanks for listening," he said. "Merry Christmas, Nurse Nelson."

"Merry Christmas," Anne said.

She watched the detective walk toward the exit. Seconds later, she stepped into the elevator and pushed the button for the pediatric intensive care unit. She needed to pick up her coat. She also wanted to check on Sally one more time.

When Anne reached Sally's room, she saw the bed was empty. "Oh, no," she thought, fearing the worst. She rushed down the hall toward the nurses' station. Her pace quickened with each step.

"Where's Sally?" she asked the unit secretary, her eyes pleading. "She's not in her room. Is she okay?"

Before the secretary could answer, Anne heard a child's laughter and Sally's voice coming from a room just across from the nurses' station. Turning, Anne felt the relief surge through her. Walking toward the room, she saw Sally reading a Christmas book to a smaller child. Another nurse stood nearby, smiling at both children. Noticing Anne, the other nurse came toward her and whispered, "Sally asked me if she could read a book to one of the younger kids. She told me that Santa told her to do something good with her new heart."

Anne lingered in the doorway for a moment, just watching Sally and the little girl. Sally looked up from the book, saw Anne, waved and smiled. Anne returned the wave and winked at Sally. Then Anne touched the other nurse on the shoulder and said, "Thank you, Linda." Seconds later, she walked alone toward the elevator.

Outside, in the hospital parking lot, Anne pulled her red wool coat tight against the cold and the wind. Inside the car, she turned on the heater and the radio, shivering until the warmth started to reach her. As she drove along the snow-lined streets toward her neighborhood, a radio station played *Silent Night*. When she heard the lyrics, "All is calm," she smiled to herself. It wasn't the way she would have described her twelve-hour shift.

Exhaustion began to overwhelm her. So did emotion as she made the last turn into her neighborhood. Her thoughts shifted to her husband, to the evergreens, to the star—to the belief that she and Jeff would always be together. Nearing her house, it hit her all at once. Tears streamed down her face so fast that she stopped the car in the middle of the snow-covered street. She just sat there, shaking uncontrollably, until the blare of a car's horn from the opposite direction jolted her. When she looked up, the snow began to fall softly again. She wiped her eyes and her face with her hands. Then she pulled her car carefully to the side of the street so the other driver could pass. That's when she first noticed it. She just wasn't sure that what she saw was real. She wondered if it was a mirage from the snow and the glow of the streetlights. She got out of her car and just stood there in awe. Then she started running toward her front yard.

When she stopped, she stood just inches from a small evergreen tree decorated with white lights and topped with a brilliant white star. Looking at the other trees in the yard, she knew this one wasn't there when she left for work this morning. The small, newly-planted tree glowed beyond its size against the backdrop of her dark house and the moonless night.

The sight of the small, lit tree reminded her immediately of Jeff and their first Christmas together. She remembered how he asked her to close her eyes and hold his hand as they walked from their front door into the early morning darkness. She recalled how their steps crunched in the snow, how he held her as he told her to open her eyes, and how she hugged him tightly when she saw the glowing tree. She also remembered him saying, "The star will be our sign of hope every year, no matter what happens."

Looking at this new tree, Anne held her right hand across her mouth and shook her head in wonder. She noticed an envelope wrapped in gold ribbon at the base of the tree. She knelt in the snow to reach it. Opening the envelope, she unfolded a note and read:

"Dear Anne,

"I started this morning believing I had one more gift to give. I just wasn't sure what the gift was or whom I should give it to. Now, I just want to thank you for the gift you gave me today, by taking me to Sally and by doing everything you could to help the baby live. Thank you for giving hope to Katie, Joe, Jack, and me. All of us desperately needed it. You gave light to our darkness. We wanted to remind you of that feeling, too. He is with you always, Anne. Merry Christmas.

"P. S. When you're finished reading this note, look closely at the star on the top of the tree. There's something else we wanted you to see."

Anne lowered the letter and looked up at the star. When she did, a flash of light streaked from her yard to the sky, like a comet. The light was so brilliant it illuminated the yellow cab and the tree-trimming truck just around the bend from her house. It also shined on the four people standing by her house, near an outdoor light switch. Yet Anne didn't notice them. She focused her attention on all the evergreens that glowed with white lights, shimmering in the darkness. Her eyes lit up, too. They also began to fill with tears. Then she saw Katie walking across the yard toward her, followed by Joe, Jack, and Santa. When Katie reached her, the two women hugged.

"We hope you don't mind us doing this," Jack said, putting his right hand on her shoulder. "We didn't mean to make you cry."

"We just wanted to do something special for you," Santa said. "You were there for us. We want you to know we'll be there for you."

"No, no, it's wonderful," Anne said, looking at the trees. "I'm crying because it's so beautiful."

Katie reached into her coat pocket and offered a tissue to Anne. When she finished wiping her eyes, Anne said, "Thank you. All of you. This is the first day in a long time I've had a feeling of hope."

"We know what you mean," Katie said. "It's wonderful to believe again."

Their nods and smiles showed they all shared that same thought, that same gift of Christmas. While the snow continued to fall gently, Joe reached for Katie's hand and Katie reached for Anne's. Soon all five of them stood side by side. As the lights and the stars on the evergreens beamed upon them, they held onto each other.

They held on to the gift of hope.

Christmas, A Year Later

The surprise package arrived in the mail a week before Christmas. When she saw the name on the return address, Anne wanted to open it right away but the sender had written, "DO NOT OPEN UNTIL CHRISTMAS! PLEASE!" four times on the package. So Anne placed it under the freshly cut Christmas tree she had decorated with red and silver ornaments and tinsel. During the next week, the box kept getting pushed back farther and farther as she put gifts for other people around the tree. And by Christmas morning, she had forgotten about the package, caught up in all the things she still needed to do for the Christmas dinner she had planned.

She filled the morning and afternoon of Christmas by baking cookies, cooking the ham, setting the table, and doing dozens of other items on a lengthy list that now had lines crossed through it. After putting a CD of Amy Grant's Christmas songs on the stereo, she knelt by the fireplace and struck a match. The spark set afire pages from the newspaper that soon licked flames through the dry wood.

Getting up, Anne walked toward the front window and pulled back the cream-colored drapes. Across the street, she saw six children having a snowball fight in a yard. She laughed as they kept running behind a giant inflatable snowman and a giant inflatable Santa for protection. When darkness started to sweep across the sky a few minutes later, she reached for a light switch by the front door. As she flicked it on, the evergreens in the front yard erupted in a brilliant white light, leading the children to quickly turn and look. Some even dropped their snowballs.

Anne's eyes immediately turned toward the oldest tree. In the glow of the lights, she noticed the place where the evergreen had been struck by lightning earlier in the year. The lightning strike had severed the top four feet of the evergreen, changing its shape. After it happened that spring night, Anne called Joe to look at the tree, worried about the damage to the evergreen.

"The integrity of the tree is still solid," Joe told her when he arrived early the next morning. "Its roots are strong. It won't be as perfect but it should continue to grow. You might be surprised by the shape it takes in the coming years."

Early that autumn, against the background of a breathtaking royal blue sky, Anne noticed a new branch near the spot where the lightning had struck. She focused on it now, the branch illuminated by a strand of lights and the star at the top of the evergreen.

Behind her, she heard an ornament fall from the Christmas tree in the living room. Turning, she saw the silver ball rolling to a rest near a stack of gifts. That's when she saw the "DO NOT OPEN UNTIL CHRIST-MAS! PLEASE!" package protruding from the back of the tree.

Picking it up, she walked across the room to an oak rocking chair to sit. She smiled before she even opened the package, just delighted because of who had sent it. Unwrapping the brown paper, she discovered a sleeve from a photo album. The photos showed a little girl riding a purple bike, posing in her light blue softball uniform, jumping from a diving board, and playing with her golden retriever. In all the pictures, the girl flashed a huge smile. Tears filled the corners of Anne's eyes as she looked at the photographs. The tears flowed even more freely when she found another gift inside the package: a handmade ornament in the shape of a red heart. Holding it like a precious gift, Anne read the message that came with the heart, "Merry Christmas to my favorite nurse. Love, Sally."

Placing the ornament on the tree, Anne thought about how Sally was one of the main reasons she had decided to continue working as a nurse. The other was the baby boy who had been rushed into the hospital last Christmas.

The child's struggles hadn't ended after his emergency surgery last Christmas. Anne recalled how he had come close to dying a second time just a few weeks after his birth. In all her years of nursing, she had witnessed numerous examples of courage by children facing death. But she had never seen a child fight so hard to stay alive. She thought it was almost as if the child knew how much he meant to people, how much hope he had given them. She knew that sounded crazy to think a baby could know those things. Yet she also remembered Dr. Lanzinger saying after the second near-death moment, "This child just has a will to live."

She thought about Katie and Joe during those times, too. On the day after Christmas, the young couple had returned to the hospital to sign up for the volunteer program where people hold and rock babies when their parents can't. Anne arranged for them to be assigned to the baby boy, and led them into the nursery that first day. As Katie sat on the blue cushion of a white rocking chair, another nurse brought the baby to her. The fear that had filled Katie when she found the baby in the manger had been replaced by anticipation. She reached her hands toward the child. Holding him seemed so natural, so right to her. It was everything she had hoped for when she was pregnant.

Joe watched Katie with the baby. He noticed the calm on her face, the peace. When Katie turned to look at him, he also saw the joy in her eyes. During that first visit, neither Katie nor Joe thought about what might happen when the baby's mother was found. They just focused on being there for the child. They both knew they had crossed a bridge when they poured their hearts and souls into wishing for him to live. No matter what happened this time, they believed they had the strength, the faith, and the love to face it together.

That belief was tested as the baby suffered and struggled in that first month. Still, they came every day to hold the child, to rock him, to sing him lullabies. They also stayed at the hospital around the clock the second time the child nearly died. Watching the young couple, Anne saw how much Katie had changed. The nurse even mentioned it to the young woman.

"I've noticed it, too," Katie told Anne as they stood outside the nursery. "When the baby's heart was fixed Christmas Day, it was like mine was healed, too. I just know that God is going to watch over him. And when it comes time for us to say goodbye to him, I know God will watch over us, too."

While Anne replayed that conversation in her memory, the doorbell rang. The clock chimed six times as she walked toward the door. Opening it, she saw Katie smiling at her. The two women immediately reached for each other, hugging. Then Anne turned to Joe who was just a step behind Katie. She smiled at him and said, "Merry Christmas, Joe!" as her eyes quickly shifted to the child he held.

"I can't believe how big he's getting," Anne said. "Come on, let's get all of you in here where it's warm."

Inside, Anne reached for the child who nearly died in her arms in the emergency room a year ago. Holding him, she couldn't get over the miracle that his life seemed to be. Joe and Katie felt the same way about how he had come to be part of their family.

As the baby struggled to live during his first few weeks, Detective Piersall kept trying to find the birth parents of the child. The closest he came was a phone call he received Christmas night, about an hour after he had stopped by the hospital to see if he could visit the baby. He was just ready to end his thirteen-hour day and head to his sister's house for a late Christmas dinner of leftover ham and turkey when his office phone rang. For a moment, he considered not answering it. For weeks afterward he'd wonder if he would have been better off ignoring the call.

"Hello, Detective Piersall here," he said when he picked up the phone.

The person on the other end of the call didn't say anything.

"If you want to talk, this is your chance," the detective said. "If not, I'm hanging up."

"I'm calling about the baby," a young female voice said, soft and scared. "I called all the hospitals to see if he was there. They wouldn't tell me but they gave me your phone number. They said I needed to talk to you. Can you tell me how he's doing?"

"I need to know who's calling first," Piersall said as he leaned forward on his gray metal desk. "Are you the baby's mother?"

There was silence again on the other end of the phone.

"Let's meet somewhere. We'll talk in person," Piersall said, his voice soothing, trying to gain the woman's trust.

"I can't."

"Why not?"

"Please, can you just tell me if he's all right?"

There was no doubt in Piersall's mind that he was talking to the baby's mother. He also had no doubt that the baby's condition was the only bargaining chip he had to convince her to meet him.

"I'll tell you when we meet," he said. "Where's a good place for you?"

"Please, detective," she said, crying. "I just want to know if he's alive."

This time, the silence came from Piersall's side of the call. The concern in her voice touched him. Still, he took pride in never failing to solve one of these cases. He looked at the framed awards on the wall near his desk, the awards that recognized him for being "Detective of the Year" the two previous years.

"I need to know one thing before I decide to answer you," Piersall said. "Why did you leave the baby at the church?"

"I was scared. I knew I couldn't take care of him by myself. I didn't know what to do."

"Did you know he was sick?"

"No," she said. "I never meant to put him in danger. You have to believe that. I was just hoping whoever found him would take good care of him. I thought a church was the best place for someone good to find him."

Then she paused before she asked in a whisper, "Is, is he okay?"

Piersall sighed. He looked at the only photo on his desk, a picture of him, his sister, and his parents when he was a child. He also thought of the warm smile of the nurse he had just met at the hospital.

"A young couple found him," he said, rubbing his left hand through his hair as he leaned back in his chair. "The baby nearly died before they could get him to the hospital. He had to go to surgery for his heart. But he's alive. I checked on him about an hour ago. They said he was still doing fine."

He heard her sigh in relief. "Thank you."

"Now where can we meet?" Piersall asked. "You need to be there for him. He needs his mother."

"It's too late," she said, sounding fragile and weary. "They won't let me have him back now. Not after what I did."

She hung up the phone before Piersall could say anything else. The detective never heard from her again, nor came any closer to solving the case. The next day, he went to the hospital and asked Anne if she would take him to see the baby. When she did, Katie and Joe were already in the nursery. Anne told him how they had volunteered to hold and rock the infant.

"I met them yesterday," Piersall said, watching through the nursery window as Katie sang to the child. "They seem like good people. What do you think?"

"I don't think that baby could be in better hands," Anne said.

Two months later, Katie and Joe became foster parents to the baby. By June they were allowed to adopt him. After they signed the adoption papers, Katie hugged Joe and whispered in his ear, "We're finally parents! Can you believe it?" Then she backed away from him, her hands on his shoulders as she looked into his eyes. "Of course you believe it," she said, her eyes misting. "You were the one who believed all along."

When they came home as an official family that day, they found a package by their front door, wrapped in silver Christmas paper and a royal blue bow. Opening the box, they discovered a beautiful, hand-carved Nativity set. They also found the note from Mrs. Williams that made both Joe and Katie laugh: "The streak lives! Another baby from the Live Nativity!"

Gifts come in different shapes and different forms. Some gifts, like the Nativity set from Mrs. Williams, have a destiny as a family treasure, hinting at the unusual story of how a family began. Other gifts can't be held or put on display. They exist only in the heart and the mind. Yet those presents can also represent the fulfillment of a lifelong dream. No one knew that better than the next person to approach Anne's house.

As he walked up the path to the front door, the man stopped and admired the lights of the evergreens glowing in the darkness. Then he moved closer to the smallest tree.

He smiled at the memory of helping plant it a year ago. Seconds later, he knocked on the front door of Anne's house.

"Jack!" Anne said as she opened the door.

"Merry Christmas, Anne," he said, doffing his Irish tweed cap with one hand as he held a bag of gifts in the other.

"Merry Christmas," Anne said. "Come on in. How are you?"

"Never better," Jack said, grinning.

Just as he had promised, Santa had showed up at Jack's house the Tuesday morning of his surgery. Santa also stayed in the waiting room during Jack's operation, joined there by Katie and Joe who had arrived before their daily visit to be with the baby. The surgery went well. So did Jack's recovery. Still, Jack tells anyone who will listen that the best gift he received in the past year came on the day that Katie and Joe adopted the baby. When they called him to share the news, Katie and Joe also asked Jack to be the child's godfather.

The offer thrilled Jack but he hesitated to accept.

"I'm flattered, but don't you think I'm too old for that?" Jack asked. "He needs someone younger to be his godfather."

"He wouldn't even have had a chance to live if you hadn't had the faith to give us a ride," Katie said. "We want you to be his godfather. We want you to be part of our family."

Katie's words struck at the heart of the greatest longing in Jack's life.

"Thank you," he said softly. "I would be honored."

Inside Anne's house, Jack embraced Katie, Joe, and the baby.

"How's my godson?" Jack said reaching for the child who smiled at him. Holding the boy, Jack shared the details of the conversation he had earlier that day with Santa.

"As you know, he's visiting his daughter and her family in California," Jack said. "This was the first year he got to play Santa for his granddaughter. She just turned three. He said the best part was seeing his daughter's face light up when he had the little girl on his lap. He said her look was worth the trip. He said he'll be here in spirit with us tonight. He hopes we'll think of him."

"How can we ever forget him?" Anne said.

When the phone rang in the kitchen seconds later, Anne excused herself to take the call.

"No, no, it's not an intrusion at all," she was heard saying in the other room. "I'm sure. Besides, I can't wait to see the gift you've been talking about. I'll see you soon."

Returning from the kitchen, Anne found Katie and Jack near the dining room table. The table was decorated with a white tablecloth, gold-rimmed china and an evergreen centerpiece that had a glowing candle in the middle of it. Joe had already set up a high chair, too.

"Jack was just noticing there were place settings for five people at the table," Katie said. "Is there someone else coming for dinner?"

"Yes," Anne said. "Mike Piersall. You remember him. He's the detective. The one from the hospital."

Katie smiled mischievously and turned to Jack. "He's the one who kept coming to the hospital after last Christmas, Jack. He said he came to check on the baby. As the weeks passed, I think he was there to check on Anne. You should have seen the way he looked at her."

Anne blushed.

"We're good friends right now," Anne told Jack and Katie. "We've had lunch together in the cafeteria several times. His father has Alzheimer's and sometimes Mike needs somebody to talk with besides his family. I know what it's like to lose someone you love so I've tried to help him. He's a good man and it's good to talk to him. He dropped by the hospital this week to give me a gift for you and Joe, Katie. I told you were coming to my house for dinner today. I invited him to come to dinner, too. So he could give you the gift here."

"A gift for us?" Katie said, looking confused.

Piersall knocked on the door a few minutes later. When Anne answered it, he smiled and extended a bottle of red wine toward her.

"Merry Christmas," he said. "Wow, you look beautiful."

"Thank you," Anne said, smiling. "Merry Christmas to you, too. But you didn't have to bring anything."

"That's not what C.J. said," Piersall responded. "I saw him at the nursing home today when he was giving out his gifts. I told him that I was having dinner with you and your friends. He said if I needed a gift for you, he had an extra doll."

They both laughed.

"I told him I had a gift already," Piersall said. "Then he gave me a baseball for my dad. That kid's something else."

"How was your father today?" Anne asked.

"It was a good day. I met my mom and my sister in his room. It was good to be together on Christmas."

"I'm glad," Anne said.

Inside, she introduced him again to Katie, Joe, and Jack.

"Anne said you wouldn't mind if I came for dinner," said Piersall, who held a package wrapped in shiny green paper. He turned to Katie and Joe, adding, "I just had a gift I wanted to give your family."

He handed the present to Katie, who was holding her son. Intrigued, Joe, Jack and Anne moved closer. Katie flashed a quizzical smile at Piersall before she started to carefully unwrap the gift. Finally, she opened the lid to the box. As the child reached for the gift, Katie gently removed it from the box. Jack leaned forward to see. Joe raised his camera. Anne touched Piersall's shoulder.

"Oh, my God," Katie said, looking up at Piersall. "Is this the same one?"

"Yes," the detective said. "We no longer needed it as evidence. I thought you and Joe might want it."

"I can't believe it," Katie said as she started to cry. "It's the perfect gift. Thank you so much."

Katie's fingers caressed the brown baby blanket, the exact same one her son was wrapped in a year ago. Even now, it still had small pieces of straw from the manger clinging to it. Katie held up the blanket, remembering the first time she touched it. *It's amazing,* she thought as she looked at everyone in the room. She marveled at how a Christmas scene that began with so much fear had now led to so much love.

All because of a child.

★ ★ ★

About the author...

John Shaughnessy, a writer who has made a career in the newspaper business, is best known for his uplifting stories that celebrate the humanity and dignity of all people. A graduate of the University of Notre Dame, he grew up in the Philadelphia area and now lives in Indianapolis. He is the Assistant Editor of *The Criterion,* the newspaper of the Catholic Archdiocese of Indianapolis.

John and his wife, Mary, have three children, John Michael, Brian, and Kathleen. *One More Gift to Give* is his first work of fiction.

To contact John, log on to www.onemoregifttogive.com

Acknowledgments

The inspiration for *One More Gift to Give* came from a Christmas story I once wrote for *The Indianapolis Star.* The story was a short fiction piece about a Santa Claus on Christmas morning, a story that drew from the experiences of people who have played the role. Thank you to Dennis Ryerson, *The Star's* editor, for giving permission to include an adaptation of that story in this Christmas novella. I am also grateful to Frank Espich, a photographer for *The Star,* for taking the photo of me that appears on the back cover of this book.

While writing *One More Gift to Give,* I sought input from several people. I am especially indebted to Anne Ryder and Philip Gulley—two talented individuals with generous spirits—for their insights and suggestions. I have also been blessed by the support of Carrie Newcomer, a gifted singer-songwriter, and Kerry Temple, a soulful writer-editor.

Thank you also to my publishers, Father Daniel Mahan and Jean Zander. Their enthusiasm for this book and their hard work in producing it are valued far more than they know.

A special thank you is reserved for a group of people whose influence cannot be measured or overlooked: Doris and John Shaughnessy, Anne and Eddie Erkert, Mary and Mike Minahan, Josie and Ed Lafferty, Eileen and Harry Rhea, Lillian and Tommy Goughan, and Dorothy and Al Carson. Their emphasis on family, in its many variations, is the essence of *One More Gift to Give.*

Saint Catherine of Siena Press ...

...is an Indianapolis-based publisher of inspirational and catechetical materials. You can learn more about this and other publications at:

www.saintcathpress.com

888-232-1492

✶ ✶ ✶

To order additional copies of

One More Gift to Give

call
888-544-8674

or log on to
www.onemoregifttogive.com